This is Jay.

Jay lives in a house.
It is in a village.

JAY SAVES THE DAY

BY ANNA KOPP

AN UNOFFICIAL MINECRAFT EARLY READERS STORY

For my boys, whose love of Minecraft
fuels their love of reading.

He has a bed and a chest.
What else do you see?

Jay has a farm.
He grows food to eat.

Jay also has animals.
He takes good care of them.

Jay goes to mine for gold.
He wants to make a golden sword.

He mines and mines.
He puts torches on walls.

At last he finds a cave.
He sees stone and lava.

Oh no! A cave spider!

Jay uses his stone sword.
The spider is gone! Jay wins!

Jay walks down a stone path.
Where is the gold?

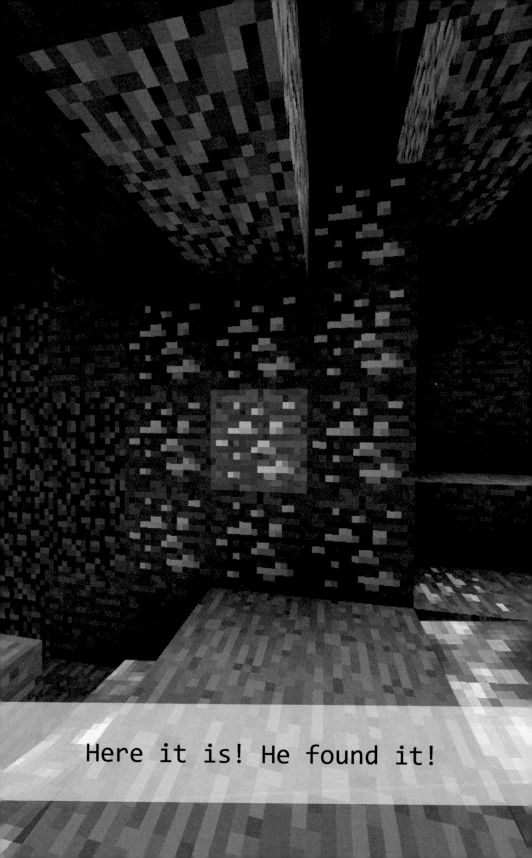

Here it is! He found it!

Jay comes back home.
He crafts a golden sword.

He looks outside.
It is dark.

Night means time for bed.

BOOM!

What was that?

"HELP!"

It is coming from the village!
Jay goes to help.

The fence is broken! Mobs get in!

Jay uses his new sword.
The mobs fall.

But there are too many.
Jay needs to fix the fence.

Jay puts in a new gate.

The mobs stop coming!

The villagers cheer!

Jay saves the day!

Made in the USA
Middletown, DE
26 October 2018